AND IN HER SMILE, THE WORLD

REBECCA J. ALLRED
GORDON B. WHITE

TREPIDATIO
PUBLISHING

ISBN: 978-1-68510-017-9 (sc)
ISBN: 978-1-68510-018-6 (ebook)
Library of Congress Control Number: 2022931589

First printing edition: February 11, 2021
Printed by Trepidatio Publishing in the United States of America.
Cover Design by Don Noble
Edited by Sean Leonard
Proofreading, Cover Layout, and Interior Layout by Scarlett R. Algee

Trepidatio Publishing, an imprint of JournalStone Publishing
3205 Sassafras Trail
Carbondale, Illinois 62901

Trepidatio books may be ordered through booksellers or by contacting:
JournalStone | www.journalstone.com

For Zach, I wouldn't change you for the world.
—Rebecca J. Allred

For Casey, whose smile turns me inside out.
—Gordon B. White

AND IN HER SMILE, THE WORLD

I.

"GO AHEAD. LET'S see some teeth," the girl says. Her name is Serena, they are in the bedroom of her apartment, and Serena wants Jeffrey to smile. She issues the command in the same cajoling tone his mother used to use when she wanted Jeffrey to think he had a choice in the matter. The voice that threatened to summon The Quiet Woman if it were not obeyed

Breathe in, a voice from memory demands, and Jeffrey instinctively obeys.

But this woman, walking slow semicircles around the foot of her bed, is not a threat. She is not The Quiet Woman whose presence is smeared around the edges of Jeffrey's childhood like a waking nightmare. She is a goddess—or will be soon, thanks to Jeffrey—and though her voice may resemble his mother's, this woman will never hurt him the way she did. After tonight, no woman will ever hurt him again.

Breathe out.

Jeffrey breathes. Smiles.

"Beautiful!" Serena crosses to the other side of the bedroom and lifts a camera, an old Polaroid almost the size of her head, from the dresser. She points it at him and presses the button. There's a flash and whirr.

"Perfect," she says, watching the image develop.

Jeffrey wants to see. It's not that he's vain, but he knows this is some kind of test and that if he passes he'll become the center of her universe.

He thinks of The Quiet Woman, crouching in the dark as he lay awake and listening to her voice late at night, and of the lies he told to convince himself she wasn't real.

Breathe in.

Jeffrey breathes in.

The girl turns her attention away from the photo and back to Jeffrey. He's sitting on the edge of her bed unrestrained, but with the exception of his facial muscles, Jeffrey is nonetheless unable to move.

Serena steps closer and says, "Now, smile harder. Wider." She smiles that other smile and adds: "Whatever you do from this point forward, don't ever stop smiling."

✳✳✳

The first rule, Jeffrey knew—even if he had never been directly told—was that you can't smile, because if you smile, you can't hide right. A smile was a crack that would inevitably spread, splitting along his teeth, opening wider until his whole face broke into laughter and the under-sink cabinet boomed like a cannon or the drapes shivered and danced around the giggling boy behind them. That was how his sister Jackie always found him, sweeping aside his concealment and shouting "Gotcha!" as fingers like pincers tweaked and poked Jeffrey, pushing him further and further into hysterical fits until the laughter warped and wracked itself into sobs. He bit down at the corners of his mouth and held his lips in a backwards pucker between his teeth.

Through thin walls and over the rush of blood in his ears, the sound of Jackie counting downstairs reached him like a radio just barely tuned back from the dial's edge.

Twelve, thirteen, fourteen.

Jeffrey glanced around his parents' walk-in closet in search of better concealment. Their room was out of bounds, but that, he had decided, was only a rule when his parents were home. When they were out and it was just he and his sister—Jackie and Jeffrey, Jeffrey and Jackie—nothing felt off-limits. Outside the closet door the great and empty bedroom offered nowhere he could think to hide, but the space behind those doors was so stuffed with secrets, he could hide forever and might never be found.

Twenty-one, twenty-two, twenty-three.

Curtains of his mother's clothes hung all around Jeffrey, the long and empty bodies dangling from hook-heads and wire shoulders while a parade of shoes marched in empty rows beneath them. Some of the hanging dresses he recognized: the black sleeveless one she wore to parties, and the black one with sleeves she'd worn to Granma Esther's funeral. There was a blue one she wore to parent-teacher night, a red one from Christmas, and several subtly different floral prints for spring and summer. But there were more, far more, than he'd ever seen—the gowns created a kind of gradient, from those familiar ones closest to the front to the ever brighter and exotic ones tucked deep in the back.

He sniffed at these, tested the musty-smelling fabric between his fingers, and found them stiff, almost grainy to the touch. Beyond these, though, hung her underclothes—snakeskin sheaths of nylon and empty bra cups staring at him like pairs of scooped-out eyes. He turned away, ears burning.

By comparison, his father's cramped corner of the closet hid like a spider's nest among flowers, the loose charcoal arms and legs of his suits drooping in their alcove. There was no color there. Even his shirts were pale whites and bloodless blues, the teeth of their buttons hanging agape and the lips of their collars slack O-shapes.

Jeffrey gave a moment's consideration to hiding in that darkness, but as he pushed aside the woolen limbs the waft of musk and sweat-stiffened wool repelled him. That's where she hides when it's light out, he thought; that's where The Quiet Woman waits for you to fall asleep.

Despite the suffocating warmth, Jeffrey shivered at The Quiet Woman's unbidden appearance in his mind. She was the one, his mother told him after the first time she caught him eavesdropping on her woman's group, who came in the night to take bad little boys and swallow them up. His mother never described The Quiet Woman, but in Jeffrey's nightmares she looked like the big bad wolf in disguise, a grandma with a mouth full of huge, silver teeth. He pushed the thought away and looked for somewhere to hide.

Twenty-nine, thirty, Jackie's voice called out. *I'm coming to get you!* Her footsteps thudded across the living room floor below, echoing through the walls and up the stairs outside the bedroom, but she was too late; Jeffrey had found a place in the corner beneath his mother's things. He let the curtain of her skirts fall over him and felt the corners of his mouth begin to draw back, but he stopped them just in time.

As he listened to Jackie's disembodied steps marking her passage through the house below—to the playroom, to the kitchen, to the mudroom; all the usual hiding spots—the heavy presence of the closet weighed on him. There was no airflow and the garments around him hung like empty lungs that sucked up all the oxygen for themselves. His eyes began to itch, his throat to tickle. For a moment, Jeffrey closed his eyes and imagined he was in the woods in summer, with the still air and the smell of the world around him and the pollen rubbing sandpaper in his eyes. Closets were magical places, were they not? He remembered how Jackie once tried to read him a story about a group of children who passed through one into a place of magic and adventure, even though he made Jackie stop because the witch in the book reminded him too much of The Quiet Woman from their mother's stories.

Jeffrey wished he could open his eyes and be in the middle of an adventure. He wished he had his own Mr. Tumnus waiting to show him the way to be the hero of his own book. To teach him how to be strong and brave like a good boy should. He almost smiled again, but swallowed it down, deep down into his tummy where he kept all the things he wasn't supposed to let out.

Outside, Jackie was getting closer—up the stairs and to the landing, across the floor outside. The floorboards chirped as she crept down the hall and stopped in front of the bedroom door. Jeffrey held his breath, taking the stale air in deep and holding it till his lungs prickled.

One, two, three, he counted, *don't smile, don't laugh, don't breathe.*

He felt as if he was going to pop, but then the floorboards beyond the bedroom sang out and Jackie crept towards their bedrooms on the house's far side. Jeffrey let the air rush out, stirring the curtain of the gold dress before his face.

Then the house shook as the front door slammed open like a fist against the frame. Even before he heard their voices, Jeffrey knew his parents were home early and their evening had not gone well. He also knew that at the far end of the house, Jackie was diving into her bed, turning off her light, and pretending to be asleep. He could almost feel the heartbeat flutter of her movements through the walls.

"I don't know why you have to ruin everything," his mother said as she pounded her way up the stairs.

"Look at this," his father yelled, his heavier footsteps trudging around the bottom floor. "Every goddamn light in the house still on. That stupid girl."

Even though Jeffrey couldn't see the lights going off one by one, he felt the timbers shudder as his father threw the switches, the electricity draining from the house as the remaining light closed like a fist around the upstairs. As it closed in around him where he still hid in their closet.

Beyond the closet, the bedroom door opened and Jeffrey heard his mother enter. Behind her, his father's heavy steps smashed into the floorboards as he climbed the stairs. Jeffrey shivered despite the stifling air and willed himself to sink into the wall, into that magic realm: Anywhere But Here.

"I should wake her up and tell her what's what," his father said as he entered.

"Just leave her alone," his mother said.

"You spoil that idiot."

His mother didn't respond.

"And the boy too," his father added.

"Maybe if he had a better role model."

Jeffrey buried himself further into the shadows. A sharp corner of something bit into his leg. Thankful for the distraction, he shuffled and pulled a wooden box out from beneath him. The top was inlaid with a rainbow; no, a smile. It was a Cheshire grin spreading its arc across the lid like a curved road paved with innumerable sharp cobblestones. Running his fingers across the image, he felt them nibble, one by one, at the ridges of each padded tip. He opened the box, the lid yawning as if breathing out, and inside he found a book.

Outside, the shouting grew louder. Jeffrey ignored it and opened the book, and—for the rest of his life—those first lines his eyes fell upon would remain brightly etched upon his memory:

And God was jealous of Creation and, wanting it for His own,
He cursed Amen and tore Her asunder.

"And why is the closet light on?" his father yelled, bringing Jeffrey back to the present. Anticipating discovery at any moment, he closed the book and put it back in the box.

"This is where your brat gets it from," his father continued.

"Oh, just shut up."

"You shut up! You don't tell me to shut up. Every time we go out, you think you can smile and flirt with every man you see."

Jeffrey wanted them to stop fighting. He wanted to leave the box behind and to make it end. He wanted to be found and for everyone to be happy and relieved they found him, so Jeffrey forced himself to smile. He forced himself to smile and then he laughed.

His father threw open the closet doors. There was Jeffrey, draped in his mother's expensive gowns and hiding with one foot loosely resting half-in and half-out of a shiny, red pump.

"What's this?" his father bellowed, grabbing Jeffrey by the shoulder and yanking him to his feet. The red shoe flew out of the closet and landed on the floor near the center of the room.

"What are you doing in there?" He smacked his son's arm, the one he wasn't gripping like a vise. "You some kind of pervert?" Another smack. "Some kind of queer?" Another.

"No!" Jeffrey bawled, although he wasn't sure what either a pervert or a queer even was.

His father slapped him once more for crying, and then he released his grip on Jeffrey, shook his head in disgust, and stomped out of the bedroom and down the stairs. Rising from the bed, Jeffrey's mother refused to meet his eye.

"Stop whining," she said as her fingernails bit into his arm. She dragged him down the hall to his room, barely stopping to sling him in and close the door. "Stop crying or *She'll* come."

Jeffrey held back the tears and looked at the marks his mother's nails had left in his arm. The little pinches of skin, bloodless white, smiled back at him like crescent moons.

✳✳✳

People used to tell Serena to smile all the time. Not ask. Tell.

The first time, she was just eleven years old. Serena was on her way home from school when a man traveling the opposite direction across the Hollie Baker Bridge, less than a mile from her house, approached her.

"Hi," the man said, crossing to the center of the bridge and effectively blocking her path.

"Hi."

"Where you going in such a hurry?"

Serena shrugged.

"Well, you can't just hurry across this bridge. Didn't you know this is a toll bridge?"

Serena knew no such thing, because the statement was a bald-faced lie. Once, the Hollie Baker River had posed a significant challenge to travelers—hence the footbridge—but years of persistent drought had long since rendered the riverbed dry. The banks were not particularly steep, and countless animal tracks crisscrossed the stony swath of earth below. Anyone who wanted to cross from one riverbank to the other could do so without the aid of the bridge, rendering it useless as a toll way.

"It wasn't this morning," she said.

The man acted as if he hadn't heard her. "You look like a smart girl. Can you guess the price for passage?"

Serena's mouth went dry as the riverbed as she debated whether to turn around and run back toward school or to kick the guy in the balls and run past him toward home. She swallowed twice and managed to say, "My mother doesn't let me carry money."

Later, she would wonder if he actually stepped closer or if she'd invented the memory, but Serena never forgot the man's breath. Not the odor, though she'd read somewhere that scent was most closely linked to memory, but the heat of it clinging to her cheeks like a damp tissue.

Serena may have been only eleven years old, but she knew she looked older than other girls her age—not a day passed that she didn't hear the boys whisper or feel the girls glare behind her back as she passed them in the hall—and Mother had warned her about the dangers of unknown men.

More than anything—more than she'd wished for Mother to win the lottery so they could move into a big house and wear nice clothes and eat something not prepared in a microwave, or for one of the Hamilton twins (Justin or Becky, didn't matter) to notice her and ask her over to watch a movie, more even than she wished for Daddy to be alive again—Serena wished she'd taken the path under the bridge. She wished she'd gone voluntarily to the dusty, rocky earth below, because she was certain she'd be there soon anyway, a film of the man's breath clinging to every inch of her rapidly cooling flesh.

"Don't look so scared," the man said. "Price of passage is only a smile." He demonstrated with unpracticed ease, revealing a set of slightly crooked teeth that couldn't have been more frightening had they been actual fangs.

Serena learned some time ago that sometimes a smile wasn't really a smile. That a real smile was organic. Involuntary. It bloomed without effort, like cherry blossoms in spring. This man's smile was not a real smile. It was unnatural—inflicted—and it seeped across his face like a bloodstain on white linen.

"I have to go," Serena said, dropping her head, making herself as small as possible, and squeezing past. When she got to the other side, she didn't run away, but she didn't exactly walk away either.

"What's your problem?" the man called after her. "I'm not a bad person. I wasn't going to hurt you. I was just trying to help you. You'd be a lot prettier if you smiled, you know!" Then quieter, but still loud enough to hear: "Bitch."

II.

"ARE YOU STILL smiling?" Serena asks, though she can see for herself that Jeffrey's smile remains plastered on his face, if not quite as widely or as brightly as before. She snaps another photo, suppressing a frown as it develops.

"There. Not bad. Not as nice as the first one, of course, but they so rarely are."

It's strange the boy is so eager to see his own picture. He's acting as though he has no interest, but she can read his desire as easily as she'd read his smile in the bar earlier that evening. He's hiding something, but she isn't yet sure if he's dangerous.

"Your teeth aren't showing in this one, teeth are important for a good smile, and your eyes reflect the light differently. No worries though. This isn't a beauty pageant."

✳✳✳

Over the years, Serena became accustomed to being measured and judged by her appearance, but it occurred in an official capacity only once.

Lips pulled back into a hideous parody of a smile, she told her mother about the unwanted advances of yet another man old enough to be her father. Mother just stood by the bed, calmly folding sheets and nodding along as if Serena were reciting Bible passages before church—as if her story were the most natural truth in the world.

When she finished, Serena expected her mother to say something. Even at sixteen, she still *needed* her to say something, to soothe the panicked animal flailing madly inside her chest. Instead, Mother sent her to her room to get started on homework. It wasn't until after dinner, as Serena helped Mother dry the last of the dishes, that Mother told her about the beauty pageant.

Serena was a far cry from a beauty queen, or so she believed, but Mother said it would be good for her, and Mother wasn't exactly a beauty queen either. Even before she'd had Serena, Mother wasn't what one might call a dainty woman; her complexion was uneven, as if the shadow of puberty had never really moved on, and her hair refused to maintain a style no matter how much time or effort was expended. Nevertheless, Mother always wore a smile and, so far as Serena had ever witnessed, never behaved as if she were anything less than a goddess. When Mother spoke, people—Serena included—obeyed.

Obedience didn't necessarily mean devotion, however, and so while Serena agreed to be in the pageant, she never pretended to like the idea.

"I don't want to do this," Serena said, a sentiment she would repeat two weeks later, framed in the bathroom mirror as Mother prepared her for the big event. Her head ached, and looking at the rows of hair twisted and tied firmly into place, she couldn't help but imagine Medusa preening before the prom. Mother promised the too-tight coils would yield a crown of stygian curls. Serena didn't know what that meant, and even though it sounded cool as hell, she wasn't interested.

"I'm well aware of your misgivings, but I assure you, this is for your own good."

"You know I'm not going to win, right?"

"Blink," Mother instructed, the mascara wand in her hand hovering less than a centimeter from Serena's right eye.

Serena blinked.

"It's not about winning."

"What's it about, then?"

Mother's own smile never faltered. "It's about remaking the world, or rather changing it, just a little. Now, show me your smile."

Serena smiled, and Mother shook her head. "No. Stop."

"What's wrong?" Serena asked, heart racing faster than she thought possible. She knew her smile lacked both the sparkle and the confidence required to impress a panel of judges, but what was the point of even trying if her own mother couldn't bear to look upon it?

A large cosmetic bag sat nearly empty on the counter, its contents strewn about the beige tiles like the remnants of an abandoned art project. Mother had moved to the adjacent bedroom where she now stood on tiptoe, reaching deep into her closet.

Serena tried again, carefully assessing her reflection. Cheeks accentuated by a fine dusting of blush firmed up like a pair of ripe cherries, and the corners of her lips, shinier and redder than even the shiniest, reddest candied apple, stretched toward the glittering teardrops that dangled from her earlobes. It may have painted her a prettier version of herself—though Serena would never admit to believing it—but the smile was a lie, and no amount of prettiness could conceal the truth.

Mother retrieved a small wooden box from inside a larger cardboard box wedged in the uppermost corner of her closet, behind a stack of old photo albums. She returned to the bathroom and sat down wordlessly in front of her daughter, the box resting in her lap.

Etched into the lid's surface, an enormous mouth grinned up at the two of them. Uneven lines gave the lips the appearance of jagged scars, and those scars stretched long and thin to opposite corners of the lid, making the smile seem impossibly wide. Impossibly wide and populated by an equally impossible number of teeth. Serena tried to count them, but every time she neared the end of the second row, she'd lose count and have to start over. Since then Serena had learned the average human mouth contained thirty-two teeth. However, she'd also learned how to be above average.

She might have sat there forever, counting the teeth in that great grinning mouth, if Mother hadn't lifted the lid and set it upside down on the counter. It was as if the lips had parted to reveal a dark, bottomless gorge—one that might demand a finger, or perhaps an entire hand, merely for peering in. It felt entirely possible that, should Serena reach inside, she'd be giving herself over to be devoured whole. It felt equally possible, however, that she would be granted a glimpse of some ancient, swallowed secret, and the temptation of forbidden knowledge was more than worth the risk.

Serena reached into the box, expecting to feel a sleeve of heat and moisture, the slick membranous throat of something still alive, but whatever she had imagined it to be, it was just a wooden box filled with pictures and religious tracts. She withdrew a stack of Polaroid photos. Beneath them was another pamphlet. She recognized that same crooked grin spread across the front and the familiar phrase in gold, shining letters: *Then you will know the truth, and the truth will set you free.*

Mother sat motionless except for her smile as Serena set the photos on the counter amidst the tubes of lipstick and foundation and gently opened the pamphlet. The inside looked like a reproduction of Genesis, and it was. Sort of. On the left side, excerpts of the old familiar text had been reprinted in red. Presented on the right and printed in the same bright gold script as the cover was an alternative story of creation.

Trembling in the darkness, He made from Her ruined form the Earth and all its mountains. Her blood became its lakes and rivers, and the oceans overflowed with Her tears. Last, He dismantled Her smile, creating from its stolen splendor the sun and the stars and all the majesty of the heavens.

Serena read the pamphlet over and over and over again, completely unaware of the new smile slowly spreading across her face.

***

Don't smile at the girls, Jeffrey's friends Russ and Toby had told him. *Don't let them know you're interested.* Girls could smell desperation in a way body spray and breath strips can't cover, and it repelled them. It was better to play it cool; smother his anxious tremors by keeping his hands in his pockets and stare at that spot between her brows instead of into her eyes. He had to be smooth if he wanted Vanessa Bridges—the only reason to go to sixth-period Chemistry—to be his date for the Fall Social.

Russ said Jeffrey must be crazy to ask her out. Did he even know her? Of course he did, although maybe only a little more than to say "Hello" to. Still, they had been part of the same lab group for a week at the beginning of the semester and she sat right next to Jeffrey in the middle of the third row. She laughed at his jokes usually, and he let her borrow a pencil or a piece of paper on more than one occasion. But even without those connections, he told Russ and Toby, he would still risk her asking out.

"Why?" Toby asked.

They were sitting at their usual table in the corner of the cafeteria. On the opposite side, over by the vending machines, the social committee had set up a table dripping with blue and gold crepe ringlets and a handmade bubble-letter sign advertising: "Fall Social – Last Day to Buy Tickets!!"

"She's got," Jeffrey paused, searching for a way to express his interest without revealing too much.

"She's got those," Russ said, then pantomimed the curve of giant breasts. "Ooh la la."

Jeffrey flushed with color, head sinking between his shoulders. "No, man, no. It isn't like that."

Vanessa was—he used the term even in his thoughts—"well-endowed," but that wasn't why he couldn't get her out of his head. He'd have been blind not to notice, but he kept his thoughts of her respectable. In fact, just a week ago, on that unseasonably warm day when the heaters in the Chemistry classroom were all blasting because they ran on timers and everyone had been sweating, basically dying, Vanessa had taken off her sweater and revealed a thin lavender tank top underneath.

Nobody could blame him for looking—boys will be boys—but when she dropped the nub of her pencil and leaned down to pick it up, the full expanse of her chest opening there before him, he'd done the right thing and looked away.

He didn't even tell anyone about it, not even Russ or Toby. He didn't even think about it when he was at home alone later that night, although he thought about thinking of it. That wasn't the kind of relationship they were going to have.

"I was going to say she's got those eyes," Jeffrey said. "And that smile. You know what I mean."

Maybe they did and maybe they didn't, but for Jeffrey that's all there was to it. The way she smiled when she spoke to the other girls, or when he loaned her a pen, or when she caught one of his jokes. It wasn't broad or wide or flat, but her cheeks pulled back more than up, so that from the corner of his eye Jeffrey could watch as the line of her pleasure drew up towards her cheek. He was only just fifteen, but he would have died for her.

"But you don't *know her*, know her, man," Russ laughed.

"And you do?" Jeffrey snapped.

"Me? No, I don't, but from what I've heard, you and I might be the only ones." Russ trailed off, his eyebrows bobbing up and down to provide the ellipsis.

"Shut the fuck up," Jeffrey said. He snaked his arm across the table, elbow plowing through the slop on his tray, grabbing at Russ's collar. "You don't know what you're talking about."

"Gentlemen." The voice of Mr. Gillespie, their English teacher, stopped them still. He took in the tableau over the bridge of his glasses, then pursed his lips. "Let's try to control our passions in public, hmm?"

"Yes, Mr. Gillespie," Toby said, pulling Jeffrey's hand away from Russ's neck. He reset their trays in a modicum of order. "Just discussing the Fall Social."

"Do it less rambunctiously, please." He left them.

Russ fumed, tugging at the distended neck of his shirt in a futile effort to straighten it. "Psycho," he muttered. "I was just telling you what I heard. You know what they say about girls with big...smiles."

"Shut up, Russ," Toby said. Although only a few months older than the others, as the first one through the closely placed gates of adolescent milestones—the first to drive, the first to grow most of a mustache, the only one who was truly a "smoker"—his voice carried extra weight.

Russ frowned, but was quiet.

"If you're going to ask her, you should do it now," Toby said, with the weary gravitas of sixteen and a half.

"I will this afternoon. In class," Jeffrey said.

"Negative, Ghost Rider," Russ said. He jerked a thumb towards the ticket table looming across the room. "Last day for tickets and when lunch is over, so's your chance. Do it now."

"I don't think—"

"Just do it already," Toby said. "I'm sick of hearing about it. Man up."

Jeffrey stood up from the table. Still seated, seemingly miles below, Russ said something and pointed across the room, but Jeffrey already knew where Vanessa was sitting.

Weaving around the tables and chairs, Jeffrey tried to keep in mind everything he had been told: *Don't smile. Man up. Be direct. Be cool. Be yourself.* Wait, who had said that last one? He stared at Vanessa in disbelief as his feet brought him closer and closer. It dawned on him that she was with a group of other girls—Tiffany, Lauren, Brooke, at least two he didn't recognize. Of course she was. And they were talking about something, something heated. Her eyes flashed; she mouthed words he couldn't hear.

Breathe in. The voice came suddenly, like a command.

He recognized the words from his sister's meditation tapes. Unsought but welcome, that memory voice stirred the same trance-inducing quietness as the one Jeffrey used to listen to through the wall his bedroom shared with Jackie's. After Mom got home from work—after she and Jackie had one of their increasingly frequent blowups—he and Jackie would retreat to the relative safety of their respective rooms. Listening to that voice had made him feel like somebody else. Somebody new and unafraid.

Breathe out, it said, and Jeffrey obliged, but his fear did not abate. Another memory coalesced. One not of a voice but of a mouth, silent but no less demanding. One ready to strip disobedient boys of their flesh with rows of silver teeth.

Breathe in.

He breathed in, taking the words into his mouth as he approached Vanessa, holding them, reshaping them, and finally returning them, simultaneously complying with the next directive.

Breathe out.

As a little boy he had found it impossible to ignore The Quiet Woman's imaginary commands. He hadn't thought of his boyhood boogeyman in years, but here she was again, and at fifteen, he was no more able to ignore her directive than when he'd been five.

Breathe in.

He breathed in.

Smile.

But boys aren't supposed to smile.

Smile or I'll eat you up.

"Yes?" Tiffany said, and the upward inflection stung Jeffrey, deflating him all at once back to where he stood beside the table. All the girls, including Vanessa, stared at him, their wet eyes glittering like stars in an alien constellation over the flat lines of their mouths.

He could feel them all speaking to each other through invisible channels, trying to decide what to do with this stranger in their midst.

"I," he stuttered.

Look at her brow, he thought, *not at her eyes.*

He fixed his gaze on the empty space above her eyes.

Now, don't let your eyes slip down to her breasts. Man up. Don't smile. Be cool. Breathe in. Breathe out.

"Jeffrey?" Vanessa smiled at him, and Jeffrey felt the gravity of that smile, the way the bow of her lips drew back but not up, pulling his gaze down like a riptide. Down to her eyes.

No, wait. Don't!

And then he saw it. The confusion and the…impatience, maybe?

Vanessa wasn't waiting for a knight in shining armor to sweep her off her feet. She didn't need a hero, or even a boyfriend. She was in the middle of a conversation, and he had interrupted her, and even though she smiled, even though from any other viewpoint it might look like she was being nice and inviting him to ask the question he'd come to ask, he could see the truth in her eyes. He was all alone, hovering like a gnat at the edge of her peripheral vision, and Jeffrey suddenly remembered something else he'd been told. Something he'd been told a thousand times but until that moment had refused to believe: *Nice guys finish last.*

Jeffrey flicked his gaze back to the empty space of Vanessa's brow. "Do you, I mean, can I," he paused. "Do you have a pencil I can borrow in sixth period?"

Tiffany laughed, but Vanessa's side-eye caught her and quieted her abruptly.

"Because you owe me," he added.

"Sure," Vanessa said, "but can I give it to you in class?" She scrunched her brow, forcing Jeffrey's eyes to bounce up from it to the ceiling and then around the room, rolling like a maniac's.

"Yeah," he said. "That's great."

The walk back to his table took ten thousand years. Behind him, Vanessa and her friends whispered and laughed, no longer even playing at concealment.

"Well?" Russ asked as Jeffrey approached. "What'd she say?"

"Shut up, Russ," was all Jeffrey could manage.

He didn't sit down. He just left the cafeteria, left his tray sitting right there by Russ and Toby, and took the long way out, past the trailers and behind the gym. He was done for today. Maybe done forever.

Jeffrey walked home beneath the brown and brittle fingers of the trees and let himself in. No one else was there, of course—his sister was at school, his mother at work. His father was wherever fathers go when they're done too. Nevertheless, Jeffrey walked slowly, almost as if trying not to wake the structure around him or whatever might be hiding in its shadows.

Up the stairs he crept, then down the hall towards Jackie's room. Inside, he was careful to keep his eyes down, lest he see anything untoward, but he rooted through her shelves and behind her photos, looking for the tape. As it continued to elude him, he grew more and more desperate, lying on the floor to search under the bed and then elbowing through the waves of garments hanging in her closet. He began to sweat.

Breathe, he tried to tell himself, but it wasn't the same.

Finally, in the top drawer of her dresser—as he very carefully moved aside her underwear, using only the tip of a finger to do it and still half-expecting a snake or some other trap hidden within the soft folds to strike him dead—he found the tape.

It must be *the* tape, he thought, because it was the only one in the entire room. He looked for a title, but the cassette appeared to be home-recorded and its cover had no logo save for a wide, hand-drawn arc like a stretched-out U. Jeffrey assumed the original recording must have belonged to one of Jackie's friends, and that she'd made a bootleg with a blank from the answering machine. The tape, like so many of his older sister's interests—cursing, smoking, industrial music—was the source of many arguments between Jackie and their mother. Jeffrey had no idea why his mother hated the recording, their arguments over this particular subject were always hushed and behind closed doors, but he had no doubt if he were caught with it, their combined wrath would swallow him whole.

Back in his room he put the tape into his old cassette player and slammed the shutter closed. *Breathe*, he told himself, mentally replaying the exercise as he placed the headphones over his ears. *Breathe in. Breathe out.*

Jeffrey hit Play, but what he heard was far from the comfort he had expected.

And God looked upon Amen, and Amen smiled. And in Her smile, God saw all that ever was or ever would be, all that was not and never could be. It contained every possible Creation. It contained both the light and the dark, and the countless motes of time that stretched forward and spiraled backward forever and ever without end. It contained God Himself—a mere observer suspended helplessly in the wonder of Amen's most glorious smile!

Then the static hissed like a serpent and instinctively, as if he might become infected otherwise, Jeffrey threw the cassette player across the room. It cracked against the wall, beyond repair—the player and the tape alike, fractured in ways that couldn't be fixed. Shards like grim plastic teeth glittered on the floor.

He half-expected The Quiet Woman to materialize from the wreckage and punish him for breaking his sister's things. When she didn't, Jeffrey hid the pieces in a sock under his bed until trash day and threw them in the can by the curb on his way to school. Later, when Jackie asked him—once, twice, repeatedly—if he had been in her room, Jeffrey just stared at the empty spot between her brows and lied.

"Okay," Jackie finally said. "But you know what happens to liars." She smiled, but it was cold and vicious. "*She* chews them up and spits them out."

For the first time in a decade, Jeffrey slept with the lights on.

III.

"CAN I SEE one?" Jeffrey asks. He's been sitting here for almost twenty minutes, and Serena is still taking pictures.

"Excuse me?"

"It's just…" He's still smiling, but Jeffrey's efforts to speak through his fixed grin have set his cheeks to quiver. "I mean you've taken a lot of pictures already. Maybe if you showed one to me, I could help you figure out why it isn't working."

Serena's eyes flash a look of incredulity, but her smile doesn't waver.

"Don't get mad. I told you, I'm one of the good guys. I'm just trying to help. It's not like either of us has ever done this before, right?"

"Right. And what exactly is it you think we're doing here again?"

For the first time since getting Serena's number from his work friend, Sara, Jeffrey begins to wonder if he's made a mistake. He pushes the thought away.

"You know," he says, because of course she knows, otherwise she wouldn't have brought him here in the first place. Serena is fucking with him. It's all part of the test, and Jeffrey isn't about to fail. His smile widens again, and he says, "The sacrifice."

✳✳✳

Judge Number Three was the first to recognize Serena's new smile.

As predicted, she hadn't won the pageant—hadn't even been in the top ten—but Serena had been awarded a small, glittering tiara and a ribbon for "Best Smile." As she stood in the hotel lobby while Mother waited just outside for the valet to return with their car, Judge Number Three, sporting an enormous, orthodontically enhanced smile of his own, commended her once more.

"Congratulations again, Serena."

"Thank you."

"It was really no contest, you know. There aren't a lot of young women these days with smiles like yours."

Warmth exploded in Serena's stomach and quickly spread to the rest of her body. She was giddy with excitement, but she also felt a bit guilty, as if she'd somehow cheated and been found out. She was about to thank the judge a third time, but at that moment Mother poked her head back into the lobby and beckoned her.

"I'll walk you out," the judge said, and followed Serena outside. He opened the passenger side door to Mother's car, but before Serena could slip inside, the judge spoke again.

"You must be very proud of your daughter."

Mother said, "Of course. What's not to be proud of?"

"I was just telling Serena how there aren't many young women these days with a smile like hers."

"Oh, I think you'd be surprised."

Serena, blinded by her unexpected victory until that moment, finally noticed that Judge Number Three's smile—though large and bright—wasn't quite right. Wasn't quite authentic. She held her breath as he leaned in closer to the two women.

"Not much about women surprises me," he said. "But you might want to be careful about where you flash those smiles of yours. Someone might notice. Someone might recognize it."

Serena looked from her mother to the judge and back again. Mother's expression didn't change. "Serena, hop in the car. We'll be leaving in just a moment."

Serena did as she was told.

Mother stood outside the car, conversing with the judge for another minute or two in a voice too low for Serena to hear, and then Judge Number Three went back inside. By the time Mother slid into the driver's seat, the atmosphere had cleared significantly. Serena tried to talk to her mother on the drive home—to coax her mother into disclosing the details of her chat with the judge, or to at least explain why he'd behaved so strangely—but all Mother would say was: "The world is full of men behaving strangely."

"Is this because of the pamphlet?" Serena finally asked. "Because of what was written inside it?"

Mother sighed. "Yes. And no." She turned to her daughter and said, "There is still a lot for you to learn, but right now isn't the time. Right now it's sufficient for you to know where you came from, that your smile is powerful, and that you must be careful, because it has the power to reshape the world."

It didn't feel sufficient, and Serena desperately wanted to know more, but she knew her mother well enough to understand that the subject was, for the time being, closed. It would remain closed for just shy of twelve hours.

Following the excitement of the pageant and the strange encounter afterwards, Serena thought she'd sleep like the dead, but the day's events only made rest more elusive. She lay awake, pondering the judge's words. What had he meant when he said someone might notice her smile? Taken out of context, the words suggested she might be discovered by a talent agent and whisked away to Hollywood where she would star in blockbuster films, date beautiful men and women, and finally give her mother the life she deserved. The tone, however, had implied something else entirely. The tone, coupled with the judge's follow-up statement, could only be interpreted as a threat.

Unable to sleep and not wanting to think any more about Judge Number Three or his cryptic innuendo, Serena got out of bed and padded down to the kitchen. She made herself a PB&J and thumbed through an issue of *Seventeen* she'd lifted from a neighbor's recycling bin the week prior. She'd already been through the magazine half a dozen times, but tired as she was, she didn't mind.

Serena finished her sandwich, went to the bathroom, and brushed her teeth again, thinking the entire time what it would be like to have so many teeth they couldn't be counted. Then, she examined her smile in the mirror. It looked the same as it always had, and yet there was also something different about it. Something she couldn't quite identify, although she knew very well the source of the change. A yawn displaced the smile, and Serena decided she'd better head back to bed. As she passed her mother's room, she noted the light was still on. She might have ignored it had she not also heard voices.

When she was younger, Serena used to sneak down the hall at night and slowly, silently crack the door to her parents' room. She'd listen to them talking, sometimes about her, but mostly about nothing. The last time she'd done this was just after Daddy had died. She crept down the hall as always, cracked the door, and listened. Mother was crying, just as Serena had expected, but when she pushed the door open a bit more to crawl inside and cry with her, Serena saw her mother sitting on the edge of the bed. She held a mirror in her hand and she was smiling the biggest smile Serena had ever seen. It nauseated her. The longer she crouched, watching Mother smile that smile and weeping at the same time, the more scared and queasy she became, so she closed the door and promptly forced it from her mind.

This time it wasn't Daddy in the bedroom with Mother, obviously, but Judge Number Three. Mother walked in a slow semi-circle around the foot of the bed, taking his picture with her Polaroid camera. She smiled as she did this, smiled and talked. The judge smiled too, but it was another of his fake grins. He was not restrained, not that Serena could see, but he nevertheless wriggled and shifted as though he were bound. After a while, the judge's face began to twitch, fatigued muscles letting his smile out bit by bit.

"You'll never get away with this," he said through gritted teeth. "I know people. People who know things. Things I don't even know!"

Mother shushed him. Then she did something Serena had never, in all her secret visits, seen her do to Daddy.

"What are you doing?" the judge asked as Mother tugged at his shoes. His voice was different now. Less angry, more uncertain.

"What does it look like I'm doing?"

Serena watched her mother strip the judge bare, neatly folding and stacking each of his removed articles of clothing on a chair beside the closet door. It was the first time she'd seen a grown man without his clothes on, and Serena was shocked to discover that it made her feel sad. Embarrassed too, but mostly just sad. If man was made in the image of God, what a pathetic creature God must be. The sadness, however, was quickly eclipsed by horror as Serena turned her attention back to her mother.

She stood before the judge, wearing nothing but that same terrible, nauseating smile Serena had secretly witnessed following the death of her father. A smile that grew wider and wider, revealing two never-ending rows of teeth. Mother's smile stretched until its corners nearly touched her earlobes.

The judge mirrored her expression, and when his smile could stretch no more, the corners of his mouth split open into ragged curves, painting his jaw with a curtain of blood. He tried to speak, but all that came out was a series of meaningless, unpronounceable vibrations. Between the flaps of his torn cheeks, Serena saw the judge's tongue writhe. Somehow she knew he was reciting the Lord's Prayer, and she waited breathlessly to see if God would answer.

In a voice not her own, through lips that did not move, Mother countered his wordless pleas with a verse both new and familiar to Serena.

"So God created mankind in His own image, in the image of God He created them; man and woman He created them. To the woman He gave the last of Amen's smile, that it might please the man, as Amen had once pleased God, and with it the ability to create new life."

As she spoke, her jaws spread apart like a python's, the dark crescent space between them expanding until Mother was blotted completely from sight.

At last the judge stirred. He gained his feet and, moving as if he'd only just learned to walk, stumbled and lurched into the waiting dark. As he passed beyond the teeth, Mother's mouth ceased expanding and proceeded to shrink back to its original size.

It happened quickly, reminding Serena of watching a film in reverse, and when it was over—when Mother looked like Mother again—the older woman doubled over and retched. Serena sprang through the door and rushed to her side.

"Mother, are you all right?"

Mother made another retching sound and went to her hands and knees.

"I'm calling an ambulance!"

Serena moved to leave, but Mother's hand shot up from the floor and clamped around Serena's forearm. She pulled Serena to the ground, drawing her in close enough to see what was emerging from between her mother's still grinning lips.

A spongy mass of bruised purple tissue bulged from her mouth. Mother heaved again, expelling more of the undulating mass.

Serena clapped her mother hard on the back. "Cough it up. It's okay. You're going to be okay."

Mother's body shook hard enough to tip a vase resting on her nightstand, and for one terrifying moment Serena was certain Mother was about to drop dead. Then she heaved one last time, and the thing slid free. It landed between Serena and her mother with a wet thud.

Mother gasped and coughed. Coughed and gasped. She released her grip on Serena and with her free hand grasped the edge of the bed, using it for balance as she rose to her feet.

Serena remained on the floor, gaping at the wad of expelled tissue. It was not quite as large as a basketball, and though its contours were smooth and somewhat rounded, the part in contact with the floor had flattened a bit. The surface rippled as if the inside were filled with something liquid. Or something alive.

Mother reached down and, cupping Serena's chin in her hand, tipped her daughter's face upward. "It's time for bed."

"What?"

"I said it's time for bed," Mother repeated.

Serena couldn't believe that after what had just happened Mother expected her to just turn around and go to sleep. "But—"

Mother shushed her the same way she'd shushed the judge a thousand years ago. "In the morning. I'm very tired right now. Please. Go to bed."

Serena didn't know what else to do, so she went to bed. The last thing she saw before closing Mother's door behind her was Mother stooping to the ground and gathering the placental mass into her arms like an infant.

The next morning, Serena skipped her usual routine and proceeded directly to the kitchen, where she could hear bacon sizzling and voices speaking. She half-sprinted down the hall, only to come to a stuttering halt when she rounded the corner to find Judge Number Three sitting at the counter and drinking a cup of coffee while Mother fried strips of bacon and stirred a pan of scrambled eggs.

Serena's stomach twisted into a greasy knot. The man drinking coffee looked and sounded like the judge—and before last night, perhaps he had been—but he was not the judge; she knew it instinctively. Something invisible had been fundamentally altered, so that this man was someone else entirely. There was something else too, a tension beneath his features, as if he was trying to suppress a tremor and was, for now, succeeding.

"Good morning, Serena," Mother said. "Don't worry, our guest was just leaving."

The judge tipped his head back and drained his mug before setting it down and pushing back from the counter. He nodded to Mother. "Thank you for the coffee."

"You're quite welcome."

"You ladies have a nice day," he said, his mouth offering a smile that seemed pleasant and sincere, but his eyes were fixed on something far away.

Serena stood motionless until she heard the judge's car start up outside and drive away, then she crossed the kitchen to inspect the stool where he'd been sitting. It was warm, confirming that what she'd seen hadn't been a hallucination.

"Mother?"

Serena's mother set a plate of bacon and scrambled eggs in front of her. "Eat," she said.

"I'm not hungry."

"Eat anyway."

Serena ate, and as she did, Mother left the kitchen and came back a few minutes later with the wooden box and the stack of pictures she'd taken the night before. She put them on the counter next to the frying pan, opened the drawer next to the refrigerator, and retrieved a box of strike anywhere wooden matches.

Mother picked a photo up off the stack and struck a match. She touched the match to the corner of the photo and said, "Be not as you were. Be now as you are, remade."

Mother burned each of the judge's photographs one by one and stirred the remains into the eggs. Serena watched silently. She suddenly understood the real reason there were no pictures of Daddy in the house anymore but couldn't understand why, instead of feeling angry or scared, she felt only curious fascination. When all but the last picture had been destroyed, Mother spooned the mixture into her mouth, swallowing the egg-coated plastic lumps until the pan was empty. The last photograph went into the box.

"I'm sorry about last night," Mother said, closing the lid again. "But that man was too dangerous to let alone."

"Dangerous how?"

"Some people like the world the way it is now, built upon a foundation of jealousy and violence. They don't want things to change."

"Was Daddy dangerous too? Did you try to change him like you changed the judge?"

Mother didn't even flinch. She nodded.

"What happened?"

"I'm going to tell you something important, Serena, something you have to remember: Some things just are. Some things, no matter how hard you try or how bad you may wish otherwise, cannot be changed."

✳✳✳

Jeffrey woke with one arm dangling off the edge of a narrow dormitory bed and another on the curve of a woman's hip. He did the right thing, letting his erection subside before he rolled over to snuggle against her. She grunted but did not wake.

In the unfamiliar room, the early morning light fell through the curtains in a sweeping arc across her face and body. Her pink lips caught the sun, while her whorls of blonde hair were almost gray in the shade. Jeffrey ran the backs of his fingers down her arm and watched the involuntary goose flesh sprout as each little follicle clenched and raised while she stirred and murmured.

He allowed his fingers to slide down her arm, over her hand, and into the empty spaces between her own fingers. When he'd finished exploring her hands, Jeffrey traced the soft curve of the girl's belly, crawling down along the dip of her hip socket and then back up along the outside of her leg. A small unshaven patch, just above the widest part of her thigh, prickled like suede. He felt his groin unfurling and once more did the honorable thing. He stopped. Not all men were so respectful.

But it wasn't just about being respectful. This was it, Jeffrey knew. He and the sleeping woman had really connected the night before over the sapphire-blue drinks she'd downed like water and the oak burn of the ones he'd bought himself. The stale smell of their shared cigarettes still clung to her hair like an earthy perfume as he contemplated burying his face in her curls.

There was a more pressing need, however, and he craned up to search the immediate area for something to drink. Eyes landing on a quarter-full Cherry 7-Up, he grabbed it and slipped the cap off, but was disappointed not to hear the sigh of escaping carbonation. Flat. He drank it anyway and then gently placed the empty bottle on the floor so as not to wake his lover.

This was what he had been striving to achieve with all those lessons. The confidence to approach a girl with just that kind of smile. He hadn't known quite what he was looking for—it was impossible to describe to anyone else, but then last night at the Despin Room, he had seen her and he'd known.

Reflecting the green lights above, her hair had curled and twisted like snakes as he approached her through the scrum of dancing bodies. He was already whisky-bold and going further, but she was too, and she kissed him even before he saw those teeth burning like stars beneath the black light. They were already so big and they seemed to be growing. They seemed to spread out further and further until they occupied the room, gnashing in time to the music. They could chew a hole in the world and swallow every one of them in a single bite!

Jeffrey shook his head and the constellation of fried neurons fell into a different alignment. That had to have been a dream from after they'd kissed, after she'd whispered in his ear and brought him back to her place. Christ, what a sick imagination he had sometimes.

His jaw ached, the muscle that slung from beneath his mandible to the top of his skull bulging from strain. Absently, he poked at his jaw. Was he grinding his teeth again?

Her name was Jaycie, he was sure. Jaycie with the Golden Fleece. Jaycie with the Electric Smile. They had talked for hours—Jaycie and Jeffrey, Jeffrey and Jaycie—about things like music and movies and everything and nothing.

Still groggy, he looked down at the girl—the woman, he corrected himself—who lay asleep beside him. Jeffrey was already imagining telling their grandchildren about how the two had met when the idea struck him to wake Jaycie with a kiss.

He imagined himself laughing and smiling and telling the rug-rats a somewhat sanitized version of the truth. He was, after all, a gentleman. Like a gentleman, Jeffrey leaned over to gently kiss his future bride—but before he pressed his lips to hers, assuring their love would last forever, he paused. Up close he could see she had fallen asleep with her makeup still on. Her cheeks were caked pink and the edges of her lips were smeared. The darkness painted around her eyes had leaked into the sleep crust gathering in the corners and turned it to coal. Her breath carried a faint aroma of meat and sweet garbage.

It was almost enough to push him back, up and out of bed, but then her lips twisted in the memory-motion of that smile from last night. That was the smile that blinded him, drew him in, and made him the center of her Milky Way and held on fast to him through the sex and the dreams and now into the morning light.

Jeffrey pressed his dry, scaling lips to hers.

Jaycie gasped, prying open her eyes against the hold of thick, day-old mascara.

"What the shit," she said.

"Hey," Jeffrey said, rolling back to let her sit upright.

"Yeah. I mean, hey," she said, shaking her head. "It's just, wow. Hey."

"Hey," he said again. Jeffrey thought he felt something building, but his brain, not yet done sponging up endorphins or filtering toxins, had disabled all but its most rudimentary defenses. He smiled at her. "Good morning."

The girl—Jaycie, he was still very certain—sat up.

"I gotta, you know." She slid an arm out from beneath the sheet and pulled a long t-shirt from the floor. She looked at him and suddenly glowed red, as if she were Eve standing in the shade of an apple tree and for the first time ever aware of her nudity. "Could you look away, please?"

It was sweet. Jeffrey indulged her, closing his eyes and laying a hand over them. Beneath his back, the mattress shifted as Jaycie slipped out of bed. He listened to her quick movements as she dressed, but before he could peek through the weave of his fingers, he heard her light steps cross the floor and exit the bedroom. He looked up just in time to catch her leaning halfway back inside. She smiled at him, but it discharged none of the electricity it had the night before.

"So," she said, her clothed half dangling in the room and her naked half concealed behind the wall, "I have an early meeting today and I need to get, you know, ready."

He nodded dumbly. "I'll, uh, get ready too," he replied.

The girl—probably Jaycie—nodded and then withdrew completely. The door one room over whiffed shut and a bolt gently tucked itself into the lock. A moment later, water rushed through the pipes in the walls, rustling against his head.

The room was light enough for the first time since arriving for Jeffrey to really look around and observe his surroundings. Although he had been in girls' dorms before and wasn't surprised by their private messiness, he was struck by the sheer number of photographs Jaycie seemed to have accumulated. From photos taped to the walls, buckled into frames, and pinned to any surface that would hold a point, a still-life battalion of girls stared and smiled back at him. He could, if it wasn't too presumptuous, trace the timeline of the woman in the bathroom and watch her grow and change through each successive photo from a little girl to the goddess she was now.

But none of the Jaycies—or was it Jamie...or Julie...or, God forbid, Jackie—in any of those taped and pinned photos was the woman he'd made love to. She was the sum of all their future experiences, and now he was a part of her too. Realizing this, Jeffrey felt suddenly ill.

Why? the photos all seemed to ask. *What makes you worthy?*

They called on him to apologize to the 18-year-old in her high school cap and gown for being the shadow that would eventually devour the bright future reflected in her smile. They demanded he tell the 12-year-old in braces that even though her teeth will turn out well, it's a shame what the cigarettes he gave her will do to the color. They asked him to explain to her mom and dad, whom Jeffrey could identify in the photos but would never actually meet, that their little girl on the recital stage will grow up to be good on the dance floor but great in the sack. They all smiled at him, mocking him as the disappointing period at the end of an otherwise lovely story.

But no! It didn't have to be like that. It wouldn't be like that.

Jeffrey looked away from the walls, away from the accusing photographs. Beside the bed lay a white notebook held shut by an elastic strap, the tongue of a bookmark protruding from its pages. There could be something in there, he thought. A journal entry about a movie she saw or book she read. He could figure out where she liked to go and suggest they meet there, or at the very least arrange to run into her.

Jeffrey opened the book with a snap of the band and riffled through the pages. There had to be something he could use to reshape her opinion of him and make her realize how great he really was. The ideal man. Barring that, maybe he would discover some information he could hold over her, just long enough for her to get to know him. Some tidbit of gossip that he could—and then there it was.

As his eyes slid over the girl's loopy sprawling hand, Jeffrey was eight years old again, hiding in his mother's closet. He was opening a box that didn't belong to him, or to any man. He had no business knowing it, but still he recognized the incantation as one from The Cult of Creation.

Be not as you were, but be now as you are: remade.

"Hey."

Jeffrey jumped. For a moment he was fifteen again, pawing through his sister's things, and The Quiet Woman had caught him. He'd pay for his indiscretion. Jeffrey raised his eyes. There was no

Quiet Woman, only Jaycie standing in the doorway. If she noticed the book beside him on the bed, she didn't mention it.

"Hey," she said again. "I really need you to go." She smiled, close-lipped and tight, and he could feel the hollowness rattling behind it. "Please."

"Do you want me to call you later?" Jeffrey asked, but even as the words came out, he was wriggling into his pants like a reptile that had molted too soon and must climb back in.

"Sure," she said, "but my phone is dead, so maybe if you write your number down, I'll put it in when it's charged."

Jeffrey was out of bed, pulling on his socks. "Why don't you just give me yours?" he asked. He stared at her, willing her smile to change back into the one from the night before.

"I usually just call people," she said, shrugging. The false grin made her face into a plastic mask.

Jeffrey stood and picked up a pen from the desk nearest the bed. He looked around for something, some paper or scrap other than the book, betting on that one chance in a million she was being sincere. But there was nothing. Of course there wasn't, because why would there be? It was just another smiling lie like the night before and the other girls before this one, whatever her name was.

Jeffrey could play that game too. Still holding the pen, he grabbed the nearest picture, untucking it from behind the lip of the mirror. Two children so young as to be sexless held plastic watering cans with flower-shaped nozzles, grinning like idiots. On the back, written in a loose womanly hand, he read: "Trudy and Sabrina." Jeffrey flapped the photo like a wing in the still air and the girl in the doorway tensed.

"What about if I write it on the back of this?" He flattened the picture on the desk and dug the tip of the pen into the back, then scribbled gibberish spirals as if to get the pen's ink flowing.

"Is that okay?" He flipped the photo over and held the pen half an inch from the toddler's eye. One quick stab right in the paper face and he'd ruin something of hers too. "I'll just write it right here."

"Please don't," the girl said in a voice so soft it may as well have been an invisible ray. "That's my sister."

A sudden wave of disgust broke over Jeffrey and he dropped the pen on the dresser with no further harm. "I'm sorry," he said, noticing the rat's nest of ridges that drawing on the back had raised. He rubbed at them with greasy fingers, trying to erase his crime, but it refused to be undone.

"I'll just go," he finally said.

The girl kept her distance as Jeffrey made his way through the small dormitory apartment to the front door. As he left, Jeffrey stole a glance at a stack of envelopes sitting unopened on the kitchen counter. The girl's name wasn't Jaycie. It wasn't Jamie or Julie or even Jackie.

"Well, I had a great time and I really am sorry," he said, stepping into the hallway, but by the time Jeffrey turned around to tell Sabrina he really did want to hear from her again, she'd already shut the door behind him.

IV.

"SACRIFICE?" SERENA ASKS, and sets down the camera. "What do you mean, sacrifice?"

***

The rain made a Rorschach of Jeffrey's khakis as he dipped from awning to overhang, pushing on towards the Gentleman's Club on Union. The boys were apt to tease that he looked a little too excited about the evening's entertainment as the raindrops looked like little pitter-pats of pre-arousal across his flat-front Dockers. *Be cool,* Jeffrey thought. *Don't let them know you've been looking forward to this.*

Ever since graduating with his MBA, Jeffrey had been adrift. He'd moved to a city where a guy with his grades could land a decent job, and although the money wasn't great, it was good enough. He participated in a number of social programs and networking activities, all of which were mundane interest groups or simple mailing lists. The Gentleman's Club, however, was something different. It was so exclusive that he hadn't even known it existed until he'd gotten the invitation—elegant raised-lettering in Silian Rail Italic on pale nimbus stock and an unmarked key fob. Jeffrey had been skeptical it was even real, but when Jon, a frat brother from college, texted Jeffrey a few days later and confirmed the invite, Jeffrey's world was irrevocably changed.

There were a thousand labels and just as many acronyms for the men of the GC, but none of them captured the group. Locker-room talk, Jeffrey had learned, was the JV compared to the GC. The group was about finding solidarity in the company of other males; it was a united front by men and for men. They didn't judge one another; in fact, they supported each other and provided a camaraderie other relationships couldn't touch. "Wingman" was too trite a term; the men of the GC were more like knights or even a band of kings. As kings, of course, they bragged of their conquests and were encouraged to share the spoils of war via pictures, videos, numbers, or sometimes more.

They knew secrets, too, and in that way the GC was a repository for every branch of esoteric study when it came to scoring. For the most elite members, though, these were not merely methods for picking up and putting down females, but deeper mysteries about women. In fact, Jeffery's own induction came one night—after too much whisky and no prospect of an easy lay—when he was just drunk enough to talk about his mother and, in a moment of weakness, to ask their leader Reggie if he knew anything about the secret group of women. About that name: *Amen.*

Just saying the name out loud made Jeffrey nauseous. Despite his inebriation, he immediately felt as though he had said something irreparably stupid, something that would haunt him even here among the GC. But Reggie didn't laugh or give Jeffrey the side-eye.

Instead, Reggie nodded. He didn't smile, but merely rubbed a finger alongside his nose and pointed back at Jeffrey with a wink.

"There's something coming up that you should see," he had told Jeffrey, and tonight was the night.

When Jeffrey arrived at the building on Union Avenue and took the elevator to the fourteenth floor, the main lights in the GC's suite of rooms were off. It would have appeared closed to anyone not in the know, but Jeffrey fobbed himself in through the thick glass doors and was greeted by the final bars of a song straining through the walls from the conference room. A dim blade of light stabbed out into the dark hall, beckoning him forward.

Slipping inside, he was smothered by the damp air, heavy with crotch sweat and the cloying spice of aftershave. A dozen or so men in folding chairs shifted and fidgeted as they stared at the naked woman at the front of the room. Her skin glistened in the glare of the presentation lights, framed against the stark white of the blank screen behind her and the matte puddle of her discarded clothes at her feet. Her face was a pallid mask of a smile, but her chest rose and fell above shallow breaths, the waves of light rippling along the slopes of her neck and breasts. Jeffrey had evidently missed the opening act, but was right on time for the main event.

He slid into an empty chair next to one of the older members, Harry, and whispered a hello. Harry merely grunted, red eyes shifting beneath the haystacks of his brow just long enough to register Jeffrey. Jeffrey debated speaking further, but Harry tugged at the thighs of his pants with knuckles warped like grey meat pies, fidgeting higher and higher until Jeffrey looked away. At the front of the room, Reggie was unrolling a sheet of plastic wrap. Daniel, the GC's number-two, brought another folding chair out from behind the podium and placed it in the middle of the tarp. Reggie stood

REBECCA J. ALLRED & GORDON B. WHITE

and the naked woman clasped his hand in the way a magician's assistant might, her teeth shining like sequins stitched into her stiff smile as Reggie led her to her seat at the center.

"Gentlemen, we're about to begin," Reggie said once the woman was in place. "As you know, however, there are certain protocols that must be followed. Accounts to be paid and the like. Therefore, before our special guest will let us begin, we must make her a suitable offering."

Daniel took a stiff-brimmed trilby from the podium and it began to pass through the audience. Chairs squeaked and suit coats ruffled as hands went into pockets, emerging with billfolds and money clips sloppy with cash to add to the pot. Jeffrey took his own clump of pre-counted bills from his shirt pocket and counted them for the ninth time since he'd left the house. He'd put them in his shirt because he had been unable to keep from touching them in his pants pocket, reaching in every few minutes to fold and unfold the wad within until he could have wrung sweat from the bills.

Paying for the girl's services wasn't a sign of weakness, as the men of the GC all knew. Jeffrey shivered in anticipation, thinking of what the woman in front of them, what most women, really, were willing to do if they were paid enough. He trembled again as the hat came around, already blooming with bills, and added his own contribution.

Up front, the face of the woman appeared five feet high on the projector screen hanging on the wall. The image swam in and out as Daniel, ever the technically inclined one, focused his camera on her face and fiddled with the levels. As she emerged in the highest definition, Jeffrey tried to take in every freckle on the bridge of the woman's nose, every pore on her cheeks, and every trickle of sweat running like a creek from the dark forest line of her hair. He watched one particular bead of perspiration grow fat and heavy, then push its way along her brow to skirt the socket of her blank eye and, shrinking as it ran, cut back into the channel where her closed-lipped smile pulled back instead of up. Her tongue flicked out, the pink bud catching the droplet in the corner.

Reggie took the hat and looked approvingly at the haul. He held it out to the woman, but she sat like a sculpture and the projection beside her stared out like a painting.

"Priestess," Reggie said, his voice booming in a half-serious solemnity, "we offer you this tithe. If it pleases you, give us a sign."

No movement at the front. Jeffrey held his breath.

"If you will accept it," Reggie said, "give us a smile."

All at once, it split her face, growing wider and wider, teeth exposed and lips peeling back, shining like a white fire and disrupting the image on the screen with an inscrutable moiré as the machine tried and failed to capture her smile. The walls bowed under the crowd's collective inhalation as they bore witness to the Smile of Amen.

Jeffrey was so locked on to the projection that only when Reggie's hand appeared on screen beside the woman's face did he realize the next stage of the performance had begun. Jeffrey watched as Reggie's fingers hesitantly reached out as if afraid of a shock, but when the tips touched her cheek and lightning did not strike, they began to caress her.

His fingers traced the line of her jaw, but the smile never wavered and her far-off stare was unchanging. Reggie dragged his index finger over the top of her lip and the downy fuzz visible on the magnified projection above and then kneaded her chin, pulling her lips down, making the smile wider but no less bright. As he proceeded, he pressed harder, smearing the tint on the woman's cheeks and the shade on her lips. Then pressing, pulling, rubbing his hands all over her face, circling her lips again and again, Reggie dipped a finger between them. It was just the tip, but his hand quivered.

Harry snuffled beside Jeffrey and the room echoed his snort through its many nostrils.

Now Reggie shoved his fingers over and across the innumerable teeth, the blunt digits glistening with saliva on the screen before them. Back and forth he brushed against them, harder and harder, but still as of yet afraid to enter.

"Do it," someone whispered, and Jeffrey was shocked to recognize his own voice.

Standing before them, Reggie translated the men's collective desire into a single command: "Open."

The woman did, and Reggie thrust his fingers into her mouth, moaning as he entered her.

Jeffrey watched, panting, as the fingers on the screen began rougher work. There were so many teeth up there that he could never count them all, but the fingers seemed to differentiate well enough. Finger and thumb, they pinched, latching onto a single tooth. Doubled by his blown up and blown out image, Reggie arched his back, hooked his arm, and yanked.

Reggie grunted, and the tooth tore loose from the woman's pink gums. He twisted, pulling and working it out as the long root slithered from the ragged hole.

Jeffrey's head swam through the flesh-hot room to the screen up front. Nauseous, he blinked, but when he opened his eyes the hole was gone, the myriad teeth having closed rank and left a thin shroud of bloody spittle to mark the loss. Behind Reggie, Daniel held forward a metal bowl and Reggie dropped the tooth with a skittering plink.

"Again," the roar came forth. Reggie smiled and reached into the woman's mouth again.

One by one, the men stood and approached the woman at the front of the room. One by one, they scrubbed their callused fingers across her face, her lips, and her teeth, before finally pushing them into the woman's mouth. By the time it was Jeffrey's turn, a red-black beard of blood covered her chin and ran down to pool in the dip between her collarbones. Still, the woman smiled.

Jeffrey reached out a hand, closer and closer to her cheek. *Look at the spot between her brows*, he thought, *and remember to breathe.* His fingers brushed her clammy skin.

"There's no time like your first," Reggie whispered from beside him. "Don't be shy."

It was like working clay, Jeffrey thought, as he rubbed her cheek, feeling the give of her flesh beneath. He had paid hard-earned money for her to sit here and smile while he dragged the back of his hand across her mouth and felt the limp kiss on each knuckle. This was fair, to push the tip of his finger between her lips, up along the gums. She owed him, and so Jeffrey pushed harder, sliding another finger in and another until her cheek bulged and strained.

He felt a hangnail sticking into the warm sheath of her mouth and so pushed again, relishing the sensation. He scraped his fingernail back and forth over her teeth like a washboard. They were so hard in the midst of the soft fold of flesh, but as he drew his finger over the uncountable ridge of pearls sliding away beneath his touch, his thoughts returned to an earlier time. He thought of the box he had found in his parents' closet that night when his father beat him and his mother punished him. The frustration, then, that grew into the anger. That had been the first time.

He shoved against the woman's mouth and her head rocked back, but she parted her teeth. His fingers were hot and damp in the suede of her cheeks, rubbing against her tongue, pinching and testing at her teeth. He felt her breath across his palm, her tongue rolling like a wave pulled by the many moons of her teeth. Was she speaking?

Jeffrey grabbed her by the tongue, and she stiffened. Reggie leaned forward, a hand up as if to stop him, but he did nothing.

What right did this woman have to speak? Jeffrey had paid for her, at least for tonight. He had paid for her smile, but why should he stop there? What right did she have to tell him to stop now that things had progressed so far?

He felt her tongue moving in slow, regular pulses. She was laughing, he thought at first. But no. He felt the heavy muscle move and his own muscles trembled in echo from finger to wrist to shoulder to ear, shaking his bones until he heard what she was saying in invisible movements. She was praying.

My smile is my power. With it I will remake the world. Through His sacrifice, may God's will be undone. Mother of all Creation, hear my prayer. Amen.

It wasn't just her smile now, but the smile of every woman Jeffrey had ever known. His mother and sister. The barista at Caffe Purá and the girl who tore tickets at the Varsity Theatre. Vanessa and Jaycie, every woman he'd ever fucked, and the ones he'd tried to but hadn't succeeded. The ones whose names were still raw, bleeding tattoos upon his tender soul and the ones whose names he'd never even bothered to learn at all.

Breathe, he thought, *and stare between her brows.*

Instead, he looked into her eyes and saw that even now, even at his most cruel, there was no room for him there. He was merely the next in a long line of eager participants in the banality of her degradation. Even if he could hurt her—and Jeffrey was no longer sure he could—it wouldn't make him special, but merely add to the same pain this woman had felt a million times before. Just another fist trying to bash its way into the center of a smile that could never be broken.

He let go of her tongue and the room groaned, their thirst for truer blood aroused and engorged but unsatiated. Without looking back, Jeffrey walked out of the conference room, out of the GC, and out into the night where the rain was coming down like a flood.

He was soaked by the time he reached his apartment building, but before he opened the lobby doors, Jeffrey was overcome by the sensation of being watched. He turned to peer back through the storm's beaded curtain and, for the first time since leaving home, Jeffrey saw—or thought he saw—The Quiet Woman.

Who else could it have been? Over the years he'd convinced himself The Quiet Woman was not real but a mere specter dreamed up by vicious women to torment little boys. But tonight he'd seen proof. He'd glimpsed a dark magic that, unlike listening to Jackie's tape through their shared bedroom wall, had summoned The Quiet Woman and made her flesh.

She crouched between two parked cars across the street. Jeffrey knew she'd watched him leave the GC like a coward and followed him home, slinking from shadow to shadow, laughing without sound. The Quiet Woman loved nothing more than the raw, bleeding flesh of little boys who were too afraid to grow up and act like men. Even now she was wondering how he would taste.

Jeffrey stood in the rain staring at The Quiet Woman, and she stared silently back, smiling all the while.

***

As she progressed through the end of her teens and into her twenties, men continued telling Serena to smile. In grocery stores and coffee shops. In classrooms and in clubs. Sometimes they stopped before passing her on the park bench across the street from her apartment, issuing their request despite the fact Serena sat with her headphones on and an open book in her lap. The faces changed, but the demand was always the same, and the first time she took one of these men home, he'd nearly gotten away.

After the incident with the judge, whose obituary had appeared in the newspaper only three days later, Mother had completely refused to discuss her—their—unique ability with Serena. The judge's obituary had been littered with words like "abrupt" and "unexpected." Words Serena understood to be code for "suicide." She assumed this was the reason Mother was so hesitant, so *restrained* as to seem almost ashamed of herself, but Serena saw no reason for shame. This was a path to heroism. They, and who knew how many other women, could change the makeup of men's hearts and reshape them into better people. As far as Serena was concerned, it was their duty—her duty—to find men like the judge and fix them, even if they didn't want to be fixed.

Serena used all the tools at her disposal to learn more, but there was precious little information regarding the deity named Amen or the Cult of Creation she'd supposedly inspired, and any details of one that could tap into the goddess's powers were not available to the general public. Whether or not it was a deliberate erasure by the men in charge of libraries and theology courses, the result was the same: The world at large was completely ignorant of the Goddess despite Her presence and the gifts She bestowed. If Serena wanted more information, she had to get creative.

As a result, whenever Serena brought a woman home, or conversely, whenever she went home with a woman, Serena would drop subtle hints in an attempt to start a conversation about the goddess, to see if they knew any more than she did. Most of the women were clueless. Serena wondered what would happen if she showed them one of the pamphlets; was that all it would take to make them like her? She wondered if knowledge of a thing alone was sufficient to draw it out of slumber or if something deeper was required. Some, though, smiled that secret smile, and when Serena smiled back, the surge of electricity it created was better than any orgasm. Still, if she pressed further, the women swallowed their smiles as if she were just another man on the street.

"Didn't your mother tell you?" they'd ask, but when Serena confessed to them what she had seen that night and why she needed to know how to use this power, they quickly gathered their clothes or hurried her out the door without so much as a goodbye.

The closest Serena ever got to official instruction was when she peeked in the little white journal of a woman named Sabrina. She only remembered her name because the two women had met due to a mix-up involving their nearly identical names and a shared love for Moscow Mules, and later, as they undressed each other, Serena had joked they weren't so much about to fuck as they were about to engage in a session of very strange, very meta, masturbation.

When it was over, and the two women lay tangled together in the afterglow of their mutual satisfaction, Serena began dropping her hints. The scene that played out over the period of the next twenty minutes did so in exactly the manner she'd come to expect.

"I'm going to take a shower," the other woman said. "I've got an early meeting in the morning, so I think it would be best if you were gone when I get back."

Serena nodded and began to get dressed, but as soon as she heard the water turn on in the adjacent room, she began frantically searching the woman's bedroom. It didn't take long for her to find the journal, and the pages fell open to the desired information as if by divine providence. Serena read just enough to get the gist before the water turned off again. She replaced the elastic band and slid the journal back into its hiding place. With the exception of her shoes, Serena pulled on the rest of her clothes and just managed to stumble out the door before the other woman exited the bathroom.

It was barely past midnight, so Serena went home, took a shower of her own, and then headed to a bar within walking distance of her apartment. She was back less than an hour later with Phil, an advertising consultant who promised he could change her image and her life.

That night with Phil, which Serena came to regard as her true passage into womanhood, everything started off just as it had the night she watched her mother and the judge from the hall. Serena used the Smile of Amen to paralyze the accountant. She photographed him using the old Polaroid camera she'd found in a thrift store nearly a year ago and stripped him bare, but when she bent to remove her own clothing, Serena's smiling face dipped momentarily beneath his line of sight.

Freed from Serena's smile and Amen's invisible bonds, Phil sprang from the bed and tackled Serena to the ground. Serena thought he meant to rape her, but as she readied her already expanding throat to scream, the man scrambled away, attempting to gain first his feet and then the front door.

Serena wasn't sure if it was from the smack on the floor or something else, but her mind felt simultaneously infinite and shrouded in fog. She opened her mouth to shout after the man, to furiously curse him, but the voice that came forth was not her own and the words it spoke were formed somewhere outside herself. Like an echo from the past, she heard the words her mother spoke, also in that other voice, on that night so long ago, and then all was dark.

"*So God created mankind in His own image, in the image of God He created them; man and woman He created them. To the woman He gave the last of Amen's smile, that it might please the man, as Amen had once pleased God, and with it the ability to create new life.*"

Abruptly the light returned, but it came without oxygen. Serena rocketed to consciousness, every fiber of her being consumed by a single directive: *Breathe!* She threw her head back and attempted to gasp, but her throat was clogged with something thick and ropey and alive. She heaved, and felt the thing slide up and partially into her mouth. Serena heaved again, forcing a knot of tissue past her teeth and out into the open air.

Breathe, her body screamed again, and Serena, unable to conceive of anything beyond that singular command, plunged both hands into the spongy mass. She began to tear it from her mouth one fistful at a time, but quickly discovered it was more effective to chew and spit. She heaved and chewed, chewed and spat, and at last it was out of her and Serena gulped at the air, choking and sputtering on the few remaining scraps of tissue that still clung to her teeth and lips.

Breathe.

Serena breathed.

Breathe.

When she'd regained her breath, Serena looked around at the mess she'd made. Articles of clothing and Polaroid photos were scattered like shrapnel across a floor splattered with blood and bits of flesh. Serena reached up to the bed and pulled the comforter over the mess like a TV detective pulling a sheet over a murder victim. She wouldn't allow herself to look. If she looked, she might see pieces of what had been inside the bruised-purple membranes. If she looked, she might see a miniature version of Phil the accountant, chewed and mangled. If she looked, she might see he was still alive.

There was only one person Serena could call. In less than an hour, Mother arrived with two rolls of paper towels, a bottle of carpet cleaner, and black plastic garbage bags tucked under her arm.

"What were you thinking?" Mother asked Serena after she'd finished helping her clean up. She tied up the last of the sacks and wiped her brow with the back of her arm. "No, don't answer that. It's obvious you weren't."

Serena wanted to tell her mother it wasn't her fault. That if she, Mother, had only done what she was supposed to do, if she'd shared the cult's secrets with Serena like all those other women seemed to think she ought to have done, this never would have happened.

"I was trying to do what's right."

"What's right? A man is dead."

Serena's face burned with shame. "That was an accident."

"Even if you hadn't panicked, that man still would have died. Look at these." Mother thrust the photographs at her. "Not even a hint of *Her* smile. I told you, Serena. I told you some things, some people, can't be changed."

"So what?" Serena shouted. "So what if I couldn't change him? So what if he couldn't accept the change I offered him and wound up offing himself because of it? The world would still be better off! Better to be dead than a piece of shit!"

She expected her mother to shout back. To ask her how she knew the dead man had been a piece of shit, even though she still held the evidence in her hands. Or to try and blackmail her into submission with some outlandish threat. What she didn't expect was for Mother to sit down on the edge of the bed and sigh as if defeated.

"Do you remember when you were little, and every spring we'd plant a garden?"

"Yes."

"And do you remember how before we'd sow the seeds, we made sure the soil was good and fertile so it would yield a healthy crop?"

Serena nodded.

"What do you suppose would've happened if the soil we planted our seeds in was toxic, poisonous, instead?"

"They wouldn't grow."

"And if they did?"

"The plants would be sick, probably toxic too." Serena was beginning to understand. She remembered a story from her school days about a man who killed his wife and buried her in the garden, and after that nothing would grow. Even when the wife's body had long since turned to dust, nothing but weeds and poisonous vines could take root in the earth where she'd lain.

"Now, imagine the whole planet," Mother continued, "imagine the whole universe really, is a garden. Think of the soil it's made from." Mother shook her head. "For every diseased thing you remake, more spring from the same blighted ground."

"Isn't there anything we can do?" Serena asked, becoming frantic. Over the years she'd convinced herself that she was the key to a new, better world. That the future depended entirely upon her ability to purge the ugliness. "Isn't there some way to make the soil fertile again? Can't we just remake the world from scratch?"

"When I was younger, I thought so." Mother's face became very stern. "But no."

"Why not? If everything the cult says is true, then this world has no right to exist in the first place. It was stolen! What's wrong with taking it back?"

Mother slapped her. "What you just said is blasphemy in every religion."

Serena smiled her old, fake smile. "If there is a way to destroy this world, to avenge the death of the true Creator and remake humanity in Her image, I will find it. And when I do—"

"And when you do?"

"It will be you who calls me Mother as you witness the birth of a new universe."

"Serena, please."

Serena snatched the photos from her mother's trembling hand, the one that hadn't slapped her, and gripped the older woman by the arm. She led her mother to the door and all but tossed her out.

"Thanks for helping me with the mess. I'm sorry to have bothered you so late, but don't worry, it won't happen again."

"Serena, *please!*"

Serena closed the door and waited for a knock that would never come.

For the next two years, Serena spent every free evening on the town, cruising bookshops and bars, libraries and clubs. Some nights she'd return alone, but mostly she was accompanied by one of an endless parade of beautiful boys and girls. The women, she fucked and probed for information about unmaking the world. The men fell into one of three categories: the good ones, she fucked; those who could be easily changed, she changed; and those who could not be changed, she set to fuck themselves and sent them on their way. But first, she photographed them, savoring the moment each time she told one of the immutably broken men to smile.

V.

JEFFREY GOT TO the Nabob fifteen minutes early, grabbed a stool and had a shot and a water before he texted the number he had been given for Serena. A phone chirped and wobbled against a table. The woman at the nearest two-top caught Jeffrey's eye in the sprawling mirror that ran the bar's length, smiling from behind the reflected rows of bottles as she raised her cell.

"You '*just* got here,' huh?"

"Serena, right?" Jeffrey turned to look at her directly. "You saw that?" He started to slide from his seat, but she stopped him with a cock of her head and a raised hand.

"I'll come to you," she said, still all smiles as she joined him at the bar. "I wouldn't want you to get lost on the way."

"It's just a—" he began, but stopped. "Never mind."

"No, tell me," Serena said. She raised a finger towards the bartender, a blonde with an undercut lounging at the far end of the room and checking her phone. "What was it?"

"Just a courage thing."

The bartender approached. She smiled at Serena, but it was a small and pensive thing.

"A Moscow Mule, please," Serena said.

The blonde nodded. "And your friend?"

"Just a water," Jeffrey answered.

Serena laughed, the edges of her smile splitting wide. The other woman retreated, grabbing the bottle of vodka and copper cup off the rack before retiring a respectable distance.

"I'm not one of those guys," Jeffrey said, pushing each word out slowly. "I mean, I just had a drink, and I don't need another. I don't lose control."

"I'm not one of those girls," Serena said. "I don't care. Have another."

"Really," he said. "I treat women with respect now."

"Only now?"

"I mean, no. Or yes, I'm not sure." Jeffrey bit his lip. "You've got me all flustered."

"Is it because you had that drink?"

Jeffrey glared at her and for a moment his jaw bulged under clenched teeth, but then the tension broke with a shrug. Whatever spark had flared up, he tamped down.

"C'mon. I'm kidding," she said, and punched him in the arm. "Don't be so sensitive."

"I'm trying not to," he said. "Really. It's just that I was already nervous about meeting you because Sara—"

"She works with you, right?" Serena interrupted him.

Jeffrey nodded. "She was telling me that you're great but that you can be kind of, you know." He shrugged as if chafing under a yoke and grinned like a cow.

Serena faced him squarely. Jeffrey tried to return her gaze without actually having to by staring somewhere between her brows, but Serena squinted her eyes, and he couldn't help but drop his own directly into her line of sight. She held him in her gaze, her lips pulling tight and thin below.

"I can be what?" she asked.

Jeffrey swallowed. "Intense."

The bartender placed a sweating copper mug in front of Serena, but she didn't look down or relax her glare. The bartender stood silent witness.

"I'm intense?"

"Yeah." He was practically whispering.

Then Serena laughed and a wide, open smile spread its wings and flashed at Jeffrey. "I'll take that as a compliment," she said.

Jeffrey laughed too, and the bartender followed suit. Everyone was laughing and smiling in their corner of the bar. They smiled and laughed, laughed and smiled, the combination perpetuating itself long past socially acceptable limits, as if it wasn't safe to stop.

"After that, I think I do need another drink," Jeffrey said to no one and everyone. "Give me the Double IPA, please," he said, turning to the woman behind the bar.

"You got it," she said, still smiling as she turned back to the rows of empty glasses.

Drinks in hand, Jeffrey and Serena talked their way through their common acquaintances and shared interests, dancing back and forth through topics as she led and he matched her footsteps. As an icebreaker, their mutual opinions of Sara: She was great. Then the arts: Serena loved the Brontë sisters but hated Bukowski, while Jeffrey couldn't understand why people read that chauvinist trash. Then exercise: She was training for a half-marathon and he was actually planning on joining a gym next week. Then politics: She voted Democrat, and he wouldn't even talk to Republicans. Then, after several rounds, the role of women in society: Serena had been a member of her campus feminist group and Jeffrey had recently gotten into contemporary feminist blogs.

"I donate to Planned Parenthood too," Jeffrey whispered as if it were a secret.

At some point during their banter the early evening had darkened into night and the Nabob's lights had dimmed and the music gone up. A press of bodies around them had sprung up like moist and fleshy mushrooms, folding Jeffrey and Serena in towards one another and against the bar. She pulled him along though, deeper and deeper into their intimate chat with the occasional smile over her Moscow Mules, although they grew less frequent as the night wore on.

Finally, Serena ordered one last drink and Jeffrey did too. Then just one more, and then another again.

"How about this," she said, leaning in close enough that her hot breath caressed his ear. "I'm really into religion, like really into it." She grinned. "I bet you are too."

"Actually, no." He shook his head.

"What?" she asked. "Really?"

"I don't want to talk about it," he said. "My mother was, let's just say, nontraditional in the religious sense. I'm pretty sure it fucked me up." He looked embarrassed. "Sorry, I didn't mean to get depressing."

"No, no," she said. "It's okay. I know a thing or two about fucked-up moms."

"To moms," he raised his glass.

"Fuck 'em," she said, and returned the toast.

Jeffrey laughed. "I do know something cool, though."

"Oh?"

"It's a secret."

"I promise I won't tell your mother." She smiled.

"Churches are bullshit, man."

"That's not a secret."

"I wasn't finished."

"Sorry."

"Churches are bullshit. Except," Jeffrey leaned in close enough that Serena could smell the hops and feel the alcohol burning off his breath as he whispered. "Do you know about the Cult of Creation?"

Her brows flew up, but Serena quickly clenched her face back into a tight smile. It wasn't quick enough, though. "Never heard of it," she said, but Jeffrey grinned at her with loose and sloppy lips. Despite her protestations, his smile never wavered.

"You *are* one of those girls," he said. "I can see it in your smile. And I'd do anything for you."

"One of those *women*," Serena said. "And even then, not quite." She drummed her fingers on the bar and bit the tip of her tongue, holding it hostage between her incisors.

In that moment of pause, though, the gloss in Jeffrey's eyes slipped and suddenly Serena was staring into a cold and distant fire. "I could tell people about you," he said. All around them the crowd was pressing in, but he slid still closer to her, smiling as his arm slithered along the bar and into her space. "I know men who know things about girls like you. Men who like to do things."

Serena took him in. "And you, Jeffrey, what do you want to do?"

"I'm a good guy, really," Jeffrey said. He straightened back up, chest puffed out and shoulders rolled back. "I told you, I'd do anything for you."

"Anything?"

Jeffrey smiled and nodded, head bouncing like a bolt was broken in his neck.

"Well, start by paying the tab," Serena said, flagging down the distant bartender. "And tell me, how do you feel about having your picture taken?"

VI.

"YOU SAID YOU'D do anything," Serena says. "So talk. What do you mean 'sacrifice'?"

Jeffrey smiles, for he no longer has a choice, but his eyes still broadcast his confusion. Serena instinctively grabs the camera, raises it, and snaps another picture, even as Jeffrey strains to speak.

"The sacrifice needed to remake the world. That's why I'm here, right?"

Serena freezes, camera still to her eye and the fresh photo hanging like a tongue from between pinched lips. The image of Jeffrey's perplexed smile is slowly proofing in the air.

"You brought me here to make me the center of the universe, right?" Jeffrey asks again from his statue-still pose on the bed.

Serena lowers the camera and looks Jeffrey in the eye. "Tell me what you mean."

"Is this part of the test?" he asks. Then Jeffrey sees it clearly: the befuddlement lurking behind Serena's false smile. "You don't know how, do you?"

Serena pulls the latest picture from the camera's grasp and inspects it, but still she finds nothing. Despite his smile, there's no trace of Her in these photos. All this photo does is confirm her judgment that Jeffrey is merely another unchangeable idiot whose devouring and destruction would barely register in his immediate world, but could never change—much less remake—the universe.

Unless, of course, Serena has been doing it wrong this whole time. Has she been doing *any* of it right? *Ever?*

"Spill it," she says. "I need to know what you know."

Jeffrey's breath is more forceful, building, straining now against the invisible forces that keep him bound and smiling. His nostrils flare, the muscles beneath his jaw bulge under the tooth-cracking strain as he tries and fails to push away the smile that holds him fast.

"Let me go," he says. "This was a mistake."

"I thought you were a good guy, Jeffrey. Don't you want to help me?" Serena pours on the treacle and tries to flash a pout, but the ingénue is an ill-fitting role.

Jeffrey snorts against the unseen pressure that holds him, and a vein surfaces from his forehead like a sea serpent under the strain. His temples throb as he struggles to move.

"Then it's the hard way," Serena says, and grabs the most threatening implement within arm's reach: a pair of heavy steel scissors. *Open and close, close and open*, the blades whisper as they rub against each other in anticipation. Serena throws a leg over Jeffrey, straddling him and then pushing the beak of the blades into the corner of his mouth.

"These are my people," she says, "my power. I have a right to know everything." A flick of her wrist screws the metal points into his cheek just enough to leave an indention. For now.

Jeffrey tries to spit, but unable to pucker, merely sprays the saliva. "You crazy bitch."

She spreads the scissor blades and slips one tip beneath the taut skin where Jeffrey's upper and lower lip meet. The glare in her eyes dares him to give her a reason.

"If the next words out of your mouth aren't about a sacrifice, not only will you not get what you came here for, but I'm going to make sure you never stop smiling."

The Smile of Amen's lingering power still holds him in place, so despite Jeffrey's grunts and rolling eyes, despite every wish and all his will, he cannot break from Serena's grasp. With a mighty exhale, *breathe out,* he surrenders.

"It was another one of you, one of you who did shows for money. I heard her praying." He breathes sharply as Serena corkscrews the blades that hold his lips, stretching them to the edge of breaking. "I felt her praying, I mean. Behind her smile."

"What did she say?"

Around the scissors' kiss, he tells her:

"*My smile is my power. With it I will remake the world. Through His sacrifice, may God's will be undone. Mother of all Creation, hear my prayer.*"

"Amen," they say in unison.

Serena removes her weapon from his jowl and stands. Hands on head and hip, she begins to circle the room. "Of course," she says to herself. "An eye for an eye, a tooth for a tooth. A sacrifice."

Ignoring the man behind her, she turns to the pile of Polaroids lying on the dresser beside her. Every twist and turn of Jeffrey's face is captured in the static moments, like a satellite survey of some distant planet's moon. Serena fans them, shifts them, pulls them out and scours them for some hidden detail, some sign of new life. Still, though, she sees nothing but toxic soil unfit for a new Garden of Eden.

"I'm wasting my time," she says, sweeping an arm across the dresser and hurling Jeffrey's faces in a flurry through the air. She frowns and runs her fingers through her hair, tugging at it; then she goes to her closet and pulls out the box inlaid with a smile. She sits and pours countless photographs onto the floor, flipping through them, picking them up to peer deeply as if reading invisible lines before discarding them again.

Behind her, Jeffrey calls out, "Hey, I'm still here."

She responds without looking up. "Why?"

She hasn't been paying attention to Jeffrey, and the hold of her smile has weakened enough that his smile, too, has faded. His fingers flex and retract like stiff little worms, and his toes rub against one another as the feeling returns. In his mouth, his tongue moves more freely.

"I'm sorry about that, but I can still be your sacrifice," he says to Serena's back. "I want to be your sacrifice."

"Why would I sacrifice you?" she asks, now riffling through her notes and her handwritten copy of the Smile of Amen that she has spent years cobbling together from memory. The tattered pages fly by under her fingers.

"Because I'm offering myself to you," Jeffrey says. "I told you, I'm a good person. Forget about just now—which was both our faults, really—I know how things are, like how men act and how they treat women. It's horrible, I admit that and I apologize for my gender, and myself, too, but we can fix that. I mean, you women are strong, I get that, but together we can make something better."

Serena hears the mattress springs groan in relief as Jeffrey stands, but she hunches further over the papers and pictures. His unsteady footsteps thud across the floor beneath still-stiff legs.

"You need me," Jeffrey says from above.

"No," she says. She doesn't even bother to look at him. "I don't."

Swarms of star-shaped holes still flit across his vision as Jeffrey stares down at the woman below. He's been searching for someone like Serena ever since he held the smiling woman's tongue at the GC. That night he had realized he wanted to be better—The Quiet Woman demanded that he be better—and from that moment on Jeffrey knew if he found the right woman, they could make an amazing new world. He had become better: more responsive, more malleable, whatever was needed. Just tonight he had tried so hard to be everything Serena wanted him to be at the bar, and even now, despite what she was doing, he forgave her. *He* forgave *her*!

She'd asked for the secret, and Jeffrey had given it to her. He had given her everything because he thought—no, he *knew*—she was his last hope. But it was worthless, because now she's sitting and staring at pictures of other men, refusing to even acknowledge Jeffrey. His vision of the new world they could make together recedes out into the void until there is only a single mote of light on the horizon.

"Please," he says in a final appeal. "All you need is a good man."

Serena closes her eyes and pinches the space between her brows to stave off an impending headache. "Well, if you see one on your way out," she says, "be sure to send him my way."

Jeffrey's world vanishes. The light goes out.

His hands move of their own accord.

Serena can't see the scissors as Jeffrey plunges them into her back, but she feels them punch their wicked hole between her ribs. The impact of the blow spins her half around from her seat on the floor, and she looks up over her shoulder with wide eyes. For a second, all Jeffrey can see is surprise.

Then Serena screams loud enough to pierce the sky. Her limbs flail, legs trying to run and arms scrabbling around for the handle that protrudes from her back like the nubbin of a vestigial wing, but each frenzied gesture pulls and tears more. A crimson wellspring pulses from the wound, the rivulets soaking her shirt and holding it tight against her body like a caul. Again and again she screams as she rolls along the floor.

"Stop it," Jeffrey yells. On his knees now, he tries to grab Serena and hold her down. To pin her and stop her thrashing, stop her screaming. He flips her over, face down on the sticky carpet, and presses a knee into her back. Though they are slick with blood, Jeffrey manages to wrap his fingers around the scissors. The blades tug against his grip with Serena's every frantic heartbeat and spasm as she bucks beneath him, but Jeffrey pushes a forearm against the back of her neck, driving her face into the ground. Muffled and gagging, she finally stops screaming.

Jeffrey holds the blade and hooks his arm. He pulls. With a great sucking sound, the scissors slither out of their hole.

Jeffrey slides off and rolls Serena over onto her back. He smiles as if the worst is already over, only to realize that his concept of worst doesn't begin to scratch the surface. With Serena's wound uncorked, there is nothing to stanch the blood. Every heartbeat pumps more and more of the hot red liquid onto the floor. She grows paler and paler, her movements slow. Jeffrey's one and only chance to matter is dying right before his eyes.

"She's here," Serena whispers, blood dribbling from the corners of her still-smiling lips.

Jeffrey stares at Serena's body and the burgundy pool growing beneath her. He watches as the gleam in her eyes fades, darkness closing in as if the final light from a dead star had reached him and then moved on. As if it had never existed to begin with.

He falls to his knees and clasps his hands as if to begin CPR, but the gesture seems so obviously too little and too late. It would only wring the remainder of the blood from her now completely motionless body. Instead, he does the only other thing he can think of: he bends toward Serena's face to give her mouth-to-mouth.

Breathe, a voice commands.

Jeffrey sits bolt upright. "Who said that?"

She's here.

Serena, though dead, is still smiling. At first Jeffrey thinks he's imagining the glow, but slowly it begins to brighten, and soon the smile that holds her lips is brighter than liquid starlight. It fills Jeffrey with a chilling blend of love, despair, and terror. And something else too. Envy.

Once again he's struck by the unfairness of it all. He was prepared to worship her, to sacrifice himself and die for her, to be the centerpiece of her new universe. And now look at him. Look at both of them.

Jeffrey stands, defeated, and moves to leave as Serena's smile grows brighter still. He doesn't notice when her mouth first begins to open. He doesn't notice, because hovering in the doorframe, having come to collect him at last, is The Quiet Woman.

A single quicksilver tear rolls down The Quiet Woman's cheek, leaving a trail like a comet's tail. Her uncountable teeth shimmer like mercury as the world around them begins to bend and stretch, the unstable forms straining against their borders toward Serena's still-expanding smile.

As The Quiet Woman floats across the floor towards Jeffrey, the scars that line her skin seem to dance. Here and there, pieces are missing, and the lips of those old wounds still strain towards each other like mouths that whisper the words etched into his memory from childhood: *He cursed Amen and tore Her asunder.*

"I didn't mean to," Jeffrey says, taking a step back.

Through His sacrifice, may God's will be undone.

He looks at Serena's body and the smile that stretches beyond human limits. *His sacrifice.* Serena's mouth opens. And opens. And opens. *May God's will be undone.*

Her rows of carnivorous teeth part to reveal a dimensionless void within—a fathomless nothing on the precipice of becoming everything. It is the color of murder, and the fetid stink of avarice and lingering shame burns his nostrils, but Jeffrey will not surrender to The Quiet Woman. He will not be punished for crimes that are not his fault. He had wanted to change the world until the girl spoiled it, but if Jeffrey cannot be something new then he will be nothing. Nothing for himself and—if need be—the rest of Creation.

He closes his eyes and jumps.

As he tumbles forward into the chasm of Serena's terrible throat and enters the place where neither time nor matter resides, Jeffrey is aware that he's smiling again. Perhaps his first true smile ever. It hasn't happened as he'd intended, but he still hopes to be the center of Serena's new universe after all. They'll create a world where good boys need never fear Quiet Women or girls with jaws like snakes. It will be a world where nobody hides behind smiles.

Breathe.

Jeffrey is no longer in a position to breathe—he's not in any position at all—but air chases him into the chasm that is Serena's infinite smile. Jeffrey has just enough time to wonder if she'll remember him before he is no more. Before he never was and never will be again.

Cheeks streaked with the Perseids of tears, The Quiet Woman follows Jeffrey into the void. The whole of God's Creation stretches and splits like Her smile, following swiftly upon Her heels.

ACKNOWLEDGMENTS

This book has been a long time in the making, so we'd like to thank our respective spouses for their love and support—not just for this book, but in all our creative endeavors.

We'd also like to express our sincerest gratitude to the first writing group we shared, which helped us both get up and running. We learned a lot from those Google Hangouts with our leader, Sean Hoade, and fellow scribes, including Sarah Walker, John H. Howard, and Maquel A. Jacobs.

In addition, we'd like to thank Billy Martin for his editorial guidance on an early draft. We'd also like to thank the amazing authors Richard Thomas, Sarah Read, and Tom Deady for their willingness to read the finished book before publication and offer their kind word.

Finally, our deepest thanks to the whole team that made this manuscript into a book: our publisher, Christopher C. Payne; our editor, Scarlett R. Algee; our proofreader, Sean Leonard; and Don Noble, for his excellent cover.

And, of course, thanks to you for reading. We hope ~~we made you smile~~ that you enjoyed it.

—Rebecca J. Allred & Gordon B. White

ABOUT REBECCA J. ALLRED

Rebecca J. Allred is the author of numerous short stories, including: "When Dark-Eyed Ophelia Sings" (*Nightscript Vol III*), "Lambda 580" (*A Walk on the Weird Side*) and "The Last Plague Doctor" (*Borderlands 6*). In addition to writing, she enjoys collecting books, spending sunny mornings in her backyard, and painting. Rebecca lives in central Oregon with her spouse, four cats, and one giant dog; you can follow their adventures online:

Twitter @LadyHazmat and IG: @Plagues_and_Doomsicles

ABOUT GORDON B. WHITE

Gordon B. White is the author of the horror and weird fiction collection *As Summer's Mask Slips and Other Disruptions*, as well as the novellas *Rookfield* and *And In Her Smile, The World* (with Rebecca J. Allred). A graduate of the Clarion West Writers Workshop, Gordon's stories have appeared in dozens of venues, including *The Best Horror of the Year Vol. 12*. He also contributes reviews and interviews to a number of genre fiction outlets. You can find him online at gordonbwhite.com or on Twitter @GordonBWhite.

CPSIA information can be obtained
at www.ICGtesting.com
Printed in the USA
BVHW041458070723
666900BV00004B/774